Trials of Korrasami: Fanfiction Archives

Story 1: Crashing with fate

An alternative first meeting between Korra and Asami, where Asami hits Korra with her bike instead of Mako.

Korra was still new in Republic City. Seeing as she had nothing better to do she decided to explore. The city was so big, so many people, buildings, so much life.

"Gotta hand it to Aang. This city is amazing. If only I knew where I'm going…" Korra sighed walking into the street.

"Look out!" A voice shouted.

Korra looked in the direction of the voice and before she knew it a moped crashed into her and she ended up flat across the road.

"Ouch…" Korra groaned as she sat up.

"I'm so sorry! I didn't see you!" The driver got off her moped and stood in front of Korra.

"How could you not see me?!" Korra was angry. "I was… um… I… oh…" The second she looked up lost her train of thought. The driver was a girl. And a very beautiful girl at that.

"I'm sorry. Are you hurt?" The girl touched Korra's arm and Korra blushed.

"Uhhh… Yeah…" Korra quickly got back up on her feet. "I grew up mastering bending so I'm used to getting hit around." Korra smiled as she spoke and she could see amusement on the girls face as well.

"Oh my Spirits! You're Avatar Korra!" The girl shouted.

"The one and only." Korra grinned and put her hands on her hips.

"I can't believe I ran over the Avatar. I'm so sorry." She apologized again.

"No its ok, really. I don't have a match or anything today so…" Korra looked away for a second.

"Oh yeah… You play for the Fire Ferrets. I saw your match." The girls smiled.

"You did? Oh man…" Korra's face flushed with embarrassment.

The girl laughed. "Anyway… I wanna make this up to you. How about I take you out to dinner?"

"Oh I don't know… I'm still new here so I don't know my way around all that well." Korra was embarrassed yet again.

"I see. How about you come to my place. It's easy to find." The girl took out a pen and a piece of paper and wrote the address on it. "Here."

"Thanks…" Korra smiled shyly. "Um when should I be there?"

"Tonight at seven." The girl got back up on her moped. "Oh by the way, I'm Asami." And with that she rode off.

"Asami…" Korra repeated. She stood there for a few moments and people were staring to stare at her. She quickly snapped out of it and made her way to Air Temple Island.

She was welcomed by Jinora and Ikki.

"Korra! Where have you been?" The girls ran up to her. They saw Korra was busy staring at a piece of paper and grinning like an idiot. Jinora smiled and airbended the paper out of Korra's hands and into her own.

"Hey!" Korra shouted.

"What's this? An address? Did a boy give you this?" Ikki asked smiling at Korra.

"No." Korra blushed. "It wasn't a boy. I meet this girl in the city and she ran me over by accident so she told me to come over tonight for dinner."

"A date?!" Jinora asked. Both her and Ikki looked at Korra in amusement.

"No! Of course not!" Korra looked away blushing.

"She's blushing; it is a date! Korra has a date with a girl!" Ikki shouted and flew up into the air.

"It's not a date!" Korra shouted and took back the piece of paper. "Now leave me alone. I don't know what I'm gonna wear." Korra said walking away. She could hear Jinora and Ikki giggling in the background.

Korra had only a few hours left to get ready and she still didn't know what to wear. "Damn it! Why can't I choose anything?! Why is this so hard?!" Korra fell onto her bed groaning.

"Korra? May I come in?" Korra heard Pema.

"Sure." Korra sat up.

Pema walked in and looked at Korra. She smiled and sat down next to her. "The girls told me you're having trouble getting dressed for your date with the moped girl."

"It. Is. Not. A. Date." Korra said looking away. "I'm not even into girls... I think..."

"Oh honey..." Pema could see that Korra was struggling with this. "There is nothing wrong with liking girls. Take Lin for example."

Korra looked up at Pema. "Lin? You mean Chief Lin Beifong?"

"Yes. She used to date Tenzin, but they broke up rather quickly. A few months later she started dating Kya and they've been together ever since."

"Kya? Aang's daughter?! You mean she and the Chief are..." Korra was surprised to say the least.

Pema nodded. "And we all love them and are happy for them. You shouldn't run away from your feelings Korra. Ever."

Korra nodded and smiled.

"Now then. Let's get you dressed up for your date." Pema laughed.

Korra just sighed and nodded.

A few hours later Korra arrived at the address. She was absolutely taken back. It was a giant mansion and on the front gate it was the word Sato.

Oh my Spirits. She's a Sato?! As in Satomobile?

Korra gulped as she entered and rang the bell. When the door opened Korra was once again left speechless. Asami was wearing a red silk dress. And she looked even more beautiful than before.

"You... Look... Stunning..." Korra said looking at Asami.

"Thank you. You look stunning too." Asami smiled.

Korra was wearing a blue shirt with the white water tribe symbol on the on the back, black pants, her brown boots, and her usual brown pelt was tied around her waist. Her hair was tied into a pony tail, a bit lower than usual.

"Thanks. It took me forever to get ready though." Korra grinned as she stepped in. "So your last name is Sato?"

"Yeah. Asami Sato. I'm the daughter of Hiroshi Sato. He isn't home right now because he has some big meeting." Asami spoke as she showed Korra around the house.

Wait... That means I'm all alone with her... And she looks so good in that dress... I just might lose it...

"Korra?" Asami spoke and Korra looked at her. "You ok?"

"Yeah. I'm perfect." Korra smiled.

As they ate Korra talked about her bending training, the tournament, the fact that Mako is a jerk and Bolin is a delight.

When they were finished they sat on the couch by the fire. Asami snuggled up against Korra and put her head just below Korra's chin. Korra smiled and wrapped her arms around Asami.

"You know I'm glad we had dinner tonight. Mind if we do it again some time?" Asami spoke and Korra hummed in response.

"Sure. And next time I would like to meet your parents too." Korra felt Asami shiver as she said that.

"Korra my mom is dead. She was killed by a firebender when I was little." Her voice was but a whisper.

"I'm sorry. I didn't mean to..." Korra was cut off by Asami.

"It's ok. It was a long time ago." Asami smiled a bit.

"But then how can you stand being around me? I'm the Avatar. The most powerful of all benders." For some reason Korra felt guilty.

"I don't know. My mom used to tell me stories about the Avatar when I was a kid. I just feel safe around you. It might be stupid but that's how I feel." Asami snuggled closer to Korra.

"Asami..." Korra placed her hand under Asami's chin and looked into her eyes. "In that case I'll protect you. So you never get hurt again." Asami could see the determination in Korra's eyes. She smiled and pressed her lips against Korra's.

Korra was surprised. She never kissed anyone before. But Asami's lips were so warm and soft, she couldn't pull away. It was Asami who pulled away and looked at Korra. At first Korra didn't do anything which made Asami worried that she may have crossed the line. But then her doubts despaired when Korra kissed her again. This kiss lasted longer. They kissed again and again. Each kiss more passionate than the last. Korra wrapped her arms around Asami and gently placed her down on the couch. She separated their lips, a small trail of saliva still connecting their tongues. Korra started kissing and biting Asami's neck, leaving small red marks. Asami moaned in response. Korra grinned and urged Asami to wrap her legs around her waist.

Slowly Korra traced her hands up and down Asami's thighs. Asami moaned again. "Korra..." Asami felt her self-control slipping away as Korra reached her wet panties. "Korra wait..." Asami gently pushed Korra away.

"What's wrong?" Korra asked still in her lust filled haze.

"I just... I don't think it's a good idea for us to just jump into bed after we only just meet. I thought we could take things slow." Asami looked up at Korra.

Korra took a deep breath. "Yeah sure. We can do that. And I'm sorry for jumping you like that."

"It ok. I liked it." Asami blushed and Korra did too.

They looked at each other and smiled. This was the beginning of a beautiful relationship.

Story 2: Wedding talks and dancing

Korra asks Asami to be her date to the wedding. Also the stuff that happened on the wedding after Korra and Asami decided to take the vacation.

It was the morning of the wedding. Everyone was really happy for Varrick and Zhu Li. Korra was happy too. She only had two problems. One: she had no idea what to wear for the wedding. Two: she didn't have a date for the wedding.

She could think of some solution for the first problem, but the second problem was killing her.

"What do I do? I can't ask Mako, that would just be so... awkward." Korra fell on the bed and rubbed her eyes. "Ok let's see... Who else can I ask?" Korra tried to clear her mind and when she did only one person came to her mind.

Asami.

Korra smiled to herself. Just the thought of the CEO was enough to fill Korra with new energy and happiness. She jumped off the bed, picked up her glider and flew off to Asami's mansion.

Korra landed on the balcony outside of Asami's bedroom. She opened the door and stepped in.

"Hey Asami I was wondering if you..." Korra stopped in the middle of her sentence. The moment she looked up she saw Asami wearing only a towel. Her hair was wet so Korra assumed she just took a shower. "You... Towel... Um..."

"Could you close the door? I don't wanna catch a cold before the wedding." Asami seemed completely calm about the situation.

Korra nodded and closed the door behind her. She placed her glider next to the door and turned back to Asami, who was still only in a towel. Korra blushed. True it isn't anything Korra hasn't seen before but she never saw another woman naked.

"You should... get dressed... so you don't catch a cold." Korra said this time looking directly into Asami's eyes.

"Yeah." Asami made her was to her closet and dropped the towel. She could hear Korra yelp and she turned to look at her. Korra was facing the opposite direction. "Why are you turning around? Are you embarrassed?" She asked, a hint of amusement in her voice didn't escape Korra's ears.

"It's not embarrassment. Its respect. I respect you so I'm not looking at you while you're naked." Korra tried to sound like her usual self but it wasn't easy.

"Hm… I see." Asami answered simply, seeing that Korra doesn't want to talk about it. She got dressed quickly. "You can turn around now."

Korra listened to Asami and turned around. One again she was stunned. Asami was wearing a white short sleeved shirt and a black mini skirt. Her hair was still a bit wet so Asami just let it fall down her shoulders.

Asami sat down on the bed and signaled Korra to sit down next to her. The Avatar gulped and sat down next to her friend.

"So what did you want to tell me earlier?" Asami smiled.

"I was… I was wondering if you wanted to go to the wedding with me?" Korra blushed again.

"With you? Like your date?" There was hint of surprise in her voice.

"No! I mean yes! I mean…" Korra didn't know how to respond.

"Wouldn't Mako make a better date to the wedding than me?" Asami asked.

"No way! I don't want Mako! I want you!" Korra realized how strange that must have sounded. "To be my date to the wedding I mean." She added.

"Oh… Well… Sure I don't have a date eather. I should be fun." The CEO smiled.

"Really?" Korra was a bit surprised. "You mean you'll go with me? That's awesome." Korra was so happy she jumped of the bed and floated in the air for a few moments. When her feet touched the floor again she grinned at her friend.

Asami giggled. "See you tonight then. At the wedding." Asami kissed Korra on the cheek and went downstairs. Korra felt like floating again.

But she remembered she still has to pick something to wear. She took her glider and hurried back to Air Temple Island.

Everyone could see that Korra was very happy for some reason. They decided to just let her be, since she hasn't looked so happy in a long time. When Korra returned to her room there was a package on her bed and a note next to it.

Korra,

Your father and I brought you a little something to wear for the wedding. Don't worry it's not a dress. Hope you like it.

Love, mom.

Korra put down the letter and opened the package. When she saw what was in there her face lit up with joy.

Time flew by quickly. Guests started arriving.

"Korra!" Korra heard the voice of her friend Bolin. When she turned around she saw Bolin, Mako and Opal.

"Hey guys." Korra waived.

When they approached her they looked stunned.

"Wow… Korra… You look… different…" Opal said looking at her more closely.

"But in a good way. Right bro?" Bolin added and looked at Mako.

"Yeah. Very cool." Mako responded.

Korra was wearing a dark blue coat with a pale blue undershirt. Attached to the back of her coat was a hood made of white wolf fur. She wore black pants and brown boots. Around her waist was a white wolf pelt, the tail was also still there. Her hair was tied in a small ponytail.

"You think so? Thanks man. My parents got me this." Korra said with her signature grin. "So let me guess. Bolin you're here with Opal, and Mako is playing the lone wolf."

"Look who's talking wolf girl." Mako smiled and lightly punched Korra on the shoulder.

"But I'm not alone. I have a date." Korra said beaming with pride.

"Really? Who is it?" Bolin asked all excited.

"You'll find out." Korra answered.

"Not fair. I wanna know." Bolin pouted.

Everyone laughed. Suddenly Korra looked behind them and her eyes lit up in delight. The gang looked puzzled. They turned around and saw Asami getting of the boat in her red dress.

Suddenly Opal realized something. "Wait, Asami is your date?" Everyone looked back at Korra but Korra didn't look at any of them. Her eyes were only on Asami. As Asami approached Korra didn't take her eyes off her for a second, or rather she couldn't.

Korra was completely hypnotized by Asami's beauty. Asami approached the gang and looked at Korra. "Hey, you look handsome tonight." Asami said with a smile.

Handsome! She thinks I'm handsome!

"Thank you. And you look…" Korra stopped for a moment trying to find the appropriate word.

"Snazzy?" Asami chuckled.

"I was gonna say beautiful." Korra grinned.

Asami and Korra were just standing there smiling and looking at each other. Somehow Opal was the only one who noticed what was going on. "Come on guys. The wedding is about to start." Opal hurried everyone to their seats because she wasn't sure how much sexual tension Korra and Asami could take before they start ripping clothes off each other.

The wedding was wonderful. The fireworks. The music. Everything. Korra and Asami got back to the party after discussing their vacation. They sat down at the table and started talking to each other. On the other table a bit further the ladies, Pema, Lin, Kya, Su and Senna, chatted.

"This is a really beautiful wedding." Pema commented looking around. "And I think there are gonna be more soon." She said looking at Bolin and Opal who were sitting on a bench laughing and holding hands.

"I don't know. I always figured Opal's gonna be the last of my kids to get married. But maybe I just don't wanna let her go. She's my only little girl. Also if she does get married I'm glad it's Bolin, he's a nice boy." Su smiled. "Although since we're talking about girls, Pema, you should be more worried."

"Why? Jinora has Kai but they're still way too young to get married. As far as Ikki goes…" Pema looked over at Ikki who was dancing with Huan. "Ikki is just… Ikki."

"I'm glad she got Huan to dance. Usually he's all about his art." Su smiled.

"If you ask me that boy is antisocial." Lin added.

"Look who's talking." Su laughed. As did everyone else.

Lin pouted and crossed her arms. Kya smiled. "Don't worry Lin. As antisocial as you might be I still love you." Kya kissed Lin on the cheek.

"Great." Lin still pouted but blushed a bit.

"Oh come on Lin. Loosen up. This is a party. You should be happy." Su smiled at her sister.

"I'm never happy." Lin responded taking a sip of her drink.

"You seemed pretty happy last night." Kya aid with a sly grin.

Lin choked on her drink. "Kya!" Lin blushed with embarrassment. Everyone started laughing. Lin pouted again.

"Lin homosexuality is nothing to be ashamed or embarrassed about. My son Wing is homosexual and we all love him." Su said patting Lin on the back.

"Your son is homosexual? Really?" Pema asked.

"Yeah. Wing was always such a free spirited boy. He was little bit of a troublemaker when he was younger. Luckily Wei kept him in check." Su smiled fondly.

"Sounds like a familiar sibling relationship." Lin grinned at her sister.

"Very funny Lin. Anyway I love Wing just the way he is. Same sex couples aren't that uncommon these days. Some of them get married too." That was true, lately more and more same sex couples got married.

"Speaking of marriage and homosexuality, look at that." Kya was looking at a specific couple. Everyone shifted their look towards that direction.

They could see Korra and Asami sitting next to each other. Korra whispered something into Asami's ear and Asami laughed. Korra did too.

"I think Senna is the one who should be most worried here." Su said and everyone looked at Senna.

"I'm not worried. Asami is an amazing woman. If Korra loves her then shes free to be with her." Senna was a lot calmer that everyone expected.

"Wait... You're not a bit surprised by the fact that Korra and Asami could be in love with each other." Pema asked a bit taken back by Senna.

"Not really. I always suspected there was something between the two of them. During Korra's recovery she always talked about Asami. She read her letters every night too. She was acting like a lovesick polar bear-pup. It was cute actually." Senna chucked at the memories.

"Well the kid has a right to be happy. Considering everything shes been through." Lin said looking at the two girls.

In the meantime, Korra was busy telling Asami about her childhood. "And then I froze his feet to the ground." Korra grinned. Asami laughed.

The music started playing again. "Hey Asami lets go dance." Korra stood up and offered a hand to Asami. Asami hesitated for a bit but then she took Korra's hand.

The way they danced was almost magical. It's like they were completely synchronized with each other. Like they were one person. When the dance ended they realized that everyone was looking and clapping at them. They blushed and quietly walked away to the nearest bench.

"Well that was a sight you don't see every day." Su said smiling.

"Korra never liked to dance. Honestly I'm surprised. But its good thing. Asami has a good influence on her." Senna added.

"I never noticed. Korra's outfit... It has white wolf fur. Did you give her that?" Kya asked looking over at Senna.

"Her father and I did." Senna smiled.

"It that a big deal?" Su asked, now curious.

"In our culture wolf fur is a sign of maturity. Usually it's given to the warriors of our tribe. But since Korra is the Avatar and by definition stronger than and man in our tribe we decided to give her one too." Senna explained. Su nodded. "Also white wolfs are very rare. Usually the fur is black, brown or grey, but since Korra is unique we wanted to give her something different. In the wolf world white wolfs are all alphas, the strongest of the strong."

"And look like this alpha already found herself a mate." Kya added as she looked over at the bench.

Korra was laying on the bench with her head in Asami's lap. They were smiling at each other.

Korra was telling Asami about her time in the South. About the lessons with Katara. About her time wondering around. Then Korra sat up. "And then Toph helped me get the poison out."

"Korra that's amazing." Asami smiled.

"Of course. The Avatar is the most amazing person ever!" Korra said full of pride. Korra pushed Asami playfully. Asami pushed back and Korra fell on her back on the bench. She pulled Asami down with her. "You didn't think you get the drop on the Avatar did you?" Korra laughed sitting up. Asami was currently sitting on top of Korra, with her tights at Korra's sides. Normally this position would be very intimate, but they seemed to lost in the moment to notice.

"Well it seems like this Avatar has a problem keeping her balance." Asami said with a smile.

"Very funny." Korra smiled back. Korra wrapped her arms around Asami's waist. She brought Asami closer and placed her head just above Asami's breasts. "I am balanced. As long as I'm with you I'm balanced." Asami sighed happily and wrapped her hands around Korra's neck. Once again this looked very intimate but the two didn't notice.

Korra inhaled Asami's scent. It was sweet. Like vanilla. This caused Asami to shiver a bit. Korra backed away for a bit. She looked at Asami and grinned at her. Asami also smiled. Korra touched her forehead to Asami's and stared into her eyes. Korra shifted her gaze to Asami's lips then back to her eyes.

"Asami I…" Korra was cut off by Asami's lips pressing against hers. The kiss lasted only for a brief second. But that was enough. One second was all they needed to make their feelings known to each other.

"I know." Asami whispered against Korra's lips. Asami looked into Korra's eyes. They were usually such a beautiful blue color. Now they were almost black. The look Korra was giving her was almost animalistic. This caused Asami to buck her hips against Korra's. A low groan escaped Korra's lips. "I'm sorry." Asami tried to get off her but Korra only tightened her grip.

"You have nothing to apologize for." Korra whispered.

From the look Korra was giving her Asami realized what Korra had in mind. "Your room?" Asami asked, her face growing hot as she waited for Korras answer.

Korra simply nodded. She lifted took Asami's hand and lead her away from the party.

"Ok how much do you wanna bet that after tonight there will be two less virgins in the world?" Kya asked with an amused look on her face. Everyone just stated laughing, even Lin.

In the meantime, Korra and Asami were kissing in Korra's room. Some part of them wondered if they were going too fast, but another part of them just wanted to enjoy this. For the first time in her life Korra felt complete. And so did Asami.

Asami was the first to wake up in the morning. She could feel Korras arms wrapped around her from behind, keeping her close to her body. Memories from the previous night flooded Asami's mind and she blushed deep red. She moved a bit but then felt Korra tighten her grip.

Korra planted light kisses on Asami's bare shoulder. "Morning, beautiful." Korra said between her kisses.

"Morning, handsome." Asami turned around to face Korra. Korra was smiling brightly at her. "Did you sleep well?"

"The best sleep I've had in three years. You?" Korra asked looking into Asami's eyes.

"Same." Asami replied. She noticed Korra was grinning. "What?"

"Your neck." Korra smiled.

Asami looked puzzled. She got up and looked at herself in the mirror. Her neck was covered in red marks. "Oh great. There's no way I can go out like this." Asami felt a pair of strong arms wrap around her. Then she felt herself being pulled back. Asami giggled as she fell back on the bed, with Korra above her.

"Really? That means I get to have you all to myself for the whole day." Korra smirked.

Asami blushed again and wrapped her arms around Korra's neck. They kissed for a few moments. "You will always have me. I'll always be only yours."

"And I'll always be yours." Korra replied kissing Asami again.

Story 3: With you

A bit of an alternative universe set between the ending of season 2 and the beginning of season 3. This is a story of what would happen if Korra and Asami stated realizing their feelings for each other much sooner.

Korra sighed heavily. It's been four days since the Vaatu crisis. Also four days since she broke up with Mako. Ever since then Mako has been avoiding her whenever he could, and where they were together, no matter what the situation, he would always be extremely awkward. Around Asami too. In about five days they would be back in Republic City and hopefully things will start to go back to normal.

Naga was laying against a wall and Korra was laying on her back. Bolin, Mako, Jinora and Ikki stepped out. Jinora and Ikki rushed to them as soon as the Vaatu thing was over because Jinora had a strong connection with the spirits.

"I'm bored!" Korra groaned. "Any of you up for a sparring match?" Korra looked at them.

Bolin refused silently, Mako just looked away, Ikki shrugged.

"Korra it's raining outside." Jinora said looking outside. Korra gave another deep sigh.

Then she heard a sneeze. She shifted her eyes to Asami who was sitting and looking at the scenery. Lucky for her she was still under the roof. Korra got off Naga and walked towards the engineer.

"You should go inside. You'll catch a cold like this." Korra said standing next to her. Asami sneezed again. "Too late. You already have one."

"I'm ok. I guess I just like looking at the scenery." Asami responded not looking away.

"It's just ice and water." Korra didn't see anything special since she grew up on the South.

"Yeah but its ice and water after the world nearly got destroyed." Asami sneezed again.

"Here." Korra took off her jacket and put it over Asami's shoulders. "It's not much, but it's better than nothing." Korra sat down next to her.

"Thanks." Asami looked at Korra and smiled. Korra smiled back.

Korra could see Asami was red in the face. She placed a hand over Asami's forehead. "The good news is you don't have a fever." Korra sighed in relief.

Asami put her head on Korra's shoulder and smiled. "Thanks Korra. Thanks for looking out for me."

"No problem. That's what friends do." Korra smiled back at Asami.

A few minutes later Korra noticed something. "Asami you're shaking. You really should go inside."

"I told you I don't want to." Asami looked up at Korra.

"You're so stubborn." Korra stood up and called for Naga. The polar bear-dog walked over to them then laid on the floor. Korra patted Naga on the head. Korra sat down, leaned against Naga. She pulled Asami towards her so she was currently sitting on Korra's lap. Korra wrapped her arms around her and brought them even closer. She put her jacket over them like a blanket.

"Korra what are you doing?" Asami blushed a bit.

"Well since you're too stubborn to go inside I'm gonna keep you warm. The best way to keep yourself warm is trough body heat. Plus, I'm the best firebender in the world so… That's extra body heat." Korra grinned.

"Oh… Thank you." Asami avoided eye contact.

Korra could see Asami was a bit uncounfterbale and stiff. She didn't blame her. After all both of them dated Mako, so things were bound to be a bit weird. Still Asami was her friend and Korra cared about all her friends.

Some time passed in silence, then Korra heard Asami let out a deep sigh. After that Asami relaxed in Korra's arms. Asami wrapped her arms around Korra's back and smiled.

"You're warm you know." Asami nuzzled her head into the crook of Korra's neck.

Korra chuckled. "Thank you. I try."

Asami laughed and closed her eyes enjoying the warmth. Korra noticed Asami wasn't shaking anymore, so she assumed Asami was no longer cold. She closed her eyes too. It didn't take long for them to fall asleep like that. That was the first of many times they would fall asleep in each other's arms.

Korra was the first to open her eyes. She felt something, or rather someone, laying against her. She blinked a few times and saw Asami still leaning against her. The Avatar smiled to herself placed her chin on top of Asami's head. She inhaled her scent; Asami smelled sweet, like roses and honey. Korra noticed that the two were still locked in their embrace from last night. For some reason that made her happy.

Asami shifted a bit and started to wake up. She noticed she was still in Korra's arms and smiled against Korra's chest.

"Morning." Korra said with a smile.

"Mmm... Morning..." Asami was still a half asleep.

"Did you sleep ok?" The master of four elements whispered.

"I did. You're really warm and... counfterbale. Like an Avatar pillow." Asami smiled.

"Interesting. You should advertise that. I bet you'd make a ton of money." Korra joked.

Asami laughed. "I can't do that. Because this way only I get to have you like this."

"I see. So you're being selfish? You don't want to share me?" Korra joked again.

"I don't." Asami replied.

Both of them realized how intimate that sounded and blushed deep red. They looked at each other and noticed how close their faces were. They blushed even more and Asami jumped away from Korra. Korra stood up and looked at Asami. Asami on the other hand looked away.

"But seriously thank you for staying with me." Asami said still not looking at Korra.

"No problem. Any time." Korra replied.

Korra took a step towards the CEO but Asami gasped and ran away. Korra wanted to follow her but she didn't know what to say to her. Should she apologize? But what for? Should she comfort her? Should she just leave her alone?

For the second time in a very short time Korra's emotions were all over the place.

"Damn it!" She shot a ball of fire into the air.

"Hey Korra you ok?" Bolin asked as he approached her from the other side of the ship.

"I don't know. One moment Asami was happy and smiling with me and the next she ran away from me. And I feel guilty but I don't know why." Korra was really irritated.

"Wait... You don't know?" Bolin widened his eyes.

"Don't know what?" Korra was confused.

Bolin sighed. He told Korra about everything that happened while she was gone. Korra felt terrible. She didn't know Asami was still in love with Mako. Maybe Asami wanted to get back with him and Korra was in the way so Asami ran away. Korra was even more confused. She didn't speak to eather Mako or Asami for the rest of the week.

After they got back to Republic City Korra had to face the press and Raiko. As well as deal with the spirit vines. A few days later Korra decided she had to talk to Asami. She flew to Asami's mansion.

She knocked on the door and a butler opened them. "Hello. Is Asami here?"

"Miss Sato is in her room." He replied.

"Thanks." Korra ran towards Asami's bedroom.

She knocked. "Asami? It's me."

"Come in." Korra heard Asami's voice and stepped inside. She closed the door behind her. Being in Asami's bedroom made Korra a bit nervous.

"What is it?" Asami sat on her bed. She was wearing a red silk night gown. It made Korra blush.

"I wanted to talk to you." Korra sat down next her. "Bolin told me what happened while I was away."

"So he told you I kissed Mako?" Asami asked.

"Uh… No… He told me you and him got back together… kind of… But that explains why he's so nervous around us." Korra laughed a bit. Asami did too.

"You aren't mad?" Asami asked.

"No. I mean I kissed Mako while he was going out with you so…" Korra replied still smiling.

"You what?" Asami narrowed her eyes at her.

"I'm so sorry! I thought you knew!" Korra started to panic.

"I'm just kidding. I knew a long time ago." Asami's face softened.

Korra sighed in relief. "Anyway I wanted to apologize to you. I didn't know you were still in love with Mako."

"What? Korra I…" Asami started but was cut off.

"I'm sorry. If you wanna get back together with him, I won't stop you." Korra said looking away.

"Korra!" Asami shouted and cupped Korra's face looking into her eyes. "I'm not in love with Mako and I don't want to get back together with him. I kissed him, but that was because I was just… upset and feeling lonely."

"So you aren't gonna date him again?" Korra was confused.

"No. Also I'm sorry I ran from you that morning. I shouldn't have done that." Asami gave a sad smile.

"No that's alright. I understand. But were you with me on the ship for the same reason you kissed Mako? Because you were lonely?" Korra wasn't smiling anymore.

"No! I did that because… I wanted to." Asami said blushing. "The truth is… I like you Korra… A lot." Asami started tearing up.

Korra was stunned.

"I'm sorry... You must think that's wired because we're both girls... And I understand if you don't want to talk to me again..." Asami started to cry. "I sorry... I just..." Asami was cut off by Korra's lips.

Asami's eyes widened. She was shocked at first but slowly started to kiss back. Korra wrapped her arms around Asami's waist and Asami moaned. Korra took that as a good sign. She parted Asami's lips and their tongues met. Another moan escaped Asami as she wrapped her arms around Korra's neck. Korra pushed Asami on the bed and kissed her more passionately. Suddenly Asami realized what they were doing and where this was going. She pushed Korra away.

Korra stumbled and almost fell down. She looked at Asami and she was crying and shaking. "Korra... We can't... You just broke up with Mako... I'm sorry but... Could you please leave..."

Korra wanted to stay but she knew Asami needed her space. She nodded and flew away on her glider. Korra flew back to the Island and went to her room. She fell down on her bed and groaned in frustration.

"Korra? You alright?" She heard Kya through her door.

"Go away!" Korra sounded upset.

"Korra come on. I know something's bothering you. You can talk to me." Kya tried to persuade Korra.

"Fine." Korra finally agreed. Kya stepped in and sat down next to Korra. She smiled at her. "I'm so confused Kya." Korra sighed.

"Confused about what?" Kya didn't know what was bothering her but she could tell it was a big deal.

"Me… Asami… About me and Asami… I…" Korra was really out of it.

"Wow… Kid slow down. Take a deep breath and tell me what happened." Kya smiled at her again.

Korra took a deep breath and relaxed. "Ok. Well about a little more than a week ago I broke up with Mako. And it was raining and Asami was cold so I hugged her to keep her warm. We fell asleep and the next morning it was really nice waking up with her like that. But then she ran away from me. Since then I've been so confused because I'm really starting to like her." Korra took another deep breath. "Then earlier today I went to talk to her because I thought she was still in love with Mako. But she said she wasn't and that she really likes me. Then she started crying and… I kissed her. We would have gone a lot further than that if Asami didn't stop us when she did. I just… I don't know… I wanted to kiss her and do stuff with her. But now… I'm more confused than ever." Korra sighed.

"So you're telling me that… You're falling for her. And that's bothering you?" Kya asked.

"I guess… I mean I really like her Kya. But I don't know if my feelings are my own or just because I recently broke up with Mako. The same thing goes for Asami's feelings for me. Plus, Asami and I are both girls… I just don't know how to handle this." Korra looked down.

"Korra… Do you know I found my soulmate?" Kya asked.

Korra shook her head. "Well it really is a fascinating story. We've been friends since we were kids. We were always there for each other. She started dating Tenzin and I was both happy and sad. I loved her and wanted her to be happy. But when they broke up I realized how much I loved her. When I told her that she was just as confused as you are now. But not long after that she returned my feelings. And I love her more than anything, even though our relationship has been on and off for years. But she's a busy woman and I can understand that." Kya looked at Korra.

"Wait... Childhood friends? Dated Tenzin? Busy woman? Lin?!" Korra was surprised to say the least. Kya nodded. "Really? I never would have guessed. Wow."

Kya laughed. "You know you're like the last person who found out about this. Everyone else already knows. But anyway you and Asami are more fit to be together than anyone else. And the fact you are starting to realize that is wonderful."

"But... I just said I'm confused about it. How can that be good?" Korra sighed.

"It's ok. Just talk to her." Kya patted Korra on the back.

Korra smiled a bit. "Alright. I'll try."

Kya smiled and Korra sat up. "Well I guess I'll go talk to her. Again." Korra took her glider and flew towards Asami's house. Again.

She arrived but this time she went in through the window, knowing that Asami probably wouldn't let her in otherwise. When she stepped Asami was sitting on her bed hugging her knees. Asami looked up to her. From the look on Asami's face Korra could tell she had been crying. Korra took a deep breath, put away her glider and slowly sat down next to Asami.

"Asami... I wanted to apologize. Again. I'm sorry for kissing you like that." Asami didn't look at her. "But I wanted you to know that it wasn't because I broke up with Mako and am using you as a rebound or something. I've been thinking about you a lot lately. And it was really confusing." Korra placed a finger under Asami's chin so she would look at her face. "But I finally understand. It took me a while but now I understand everything. When I kissed you I really liked it. It might have confused me even more but it also helped me understand. Kya talked to me too. After all of that I know... I really, really like you Asami. Would you be my girlfriend?"

Asami's eyes widened. It took her a while to process everything. "I... Yes... I will be your girlfriend... Korra..." Asami smiled and started crying again.

Korra smiled. "You shouldn't cry. It doesn't suit your pretty face." Korra leaned in and pressed her lips to Asami's. This time Asami responded immediately. It didn't take long for the kiss to become passionate. Korra pinned Asami to the bed but then she pulled away when Asami moaned and she realized that Asami was only wearing a bath robe. "Um... Sorry... Was that uncounfterbale?"

Asami smiled and wrapped her legs around Korras waist to keep her from moving away. Korra gasped. "Asami... Are you sure?" Asami nodded and pulled Korra in for another kiss. It was the first time for both of them, but for both of them it was perfect. And a night they would never forget.

Asami slowly opened her eyes only to see Korra lying next to her. When she noticed how naked they both were memories from last night flooded her mind. The kisses, touches, moans, and the gasps. Her thoughts were interrupted when Korra turned on her stomach and Asami saw light blue patterns on Korra's back. She didn't notice those last night. She started tracing the patterns with her finger.

"Like it?" Korra asked opening her eyes and smiling at Asami.

"I do. What is it?" Asami traced the patterns all the way down Korra's back.

"The symbol of Raava. It appeared on my back after the battle with Vaatu." Korra turned to her side and pulled Asami in for a kiss. "So... did you sleep well?"

"I did." Asami kissed Korra again. Asami sat up and brought the blanket to her chest. "We have to get up. Bolin and Mako will be here soon."

"Bolin and Mako? Why?" Asami didn't miss Korra's discomfort at the mention of Mako's name. She could understand why that was. Bringing up their ex-boyfriend after they just became girlfriends was more than a bit awkward. Korra sighed.

"Apparently there are still some things to clear up since the whole Varrick take over fiasco. Things have been a total mess at Future Industries. The guys are helping me sort things out. Well Bolin is, Mako just keeps his distance and nods. But things should be back to normal in a few more days." Asami got dressed and Korra did the same.

"So I guess I'll see you later then." Korra took her glider and was about to fly out, but Asami grabbed her wrist and pulled her in for a deep kiss. They stayed like that until they heard a knock. Korra pulled away and grinned. "See you."

"Yeah. I love you." Asami blushed.

Korra blushed too but kept grinning. "I love you too." With that she flew off.

For the next few days Korra spent more and more time with Asami. From the perspective of everyone else they were best friends, but from their point of view they were girlfriends, lovers. Korra had to sneak around at night but she didn't mind. They thought it would be a weird if they had to explain why Korra was going at Asami's place every night.

Things got a bit harder when they were on the journey across the Earth Kingdom. But being on the airship with everyone, going on another adventure, felt like things were going back to normal. Even Mako was beginning to act normal. Well Mako-normal anyway. One night Korra snuck into Asami's room.

"Korra..." Asami tried to hold back her voice as Korra kissed and bit her neck. "Korra someone will hear us." Asami pushed on Korra's shoulders and caused her to groan.

"Alright. But... can I stay here tonight? We haven't slept together for the last couple of days. I miss holding you in my arms." Korra smiled. "And I miss other things too." Korra's eyes roamed over Asami's body.

Asami licked her lips. "You can stay."

Korra smiled and embraced Asami. They fell asleep soon. The next day they arrived at Zoufu. Meeting Opal, Su, and the others was really fun. Plus, being there gave Korra and Asami the opportunity to... do the thing.

The next day Korra was practicing metalbending with Su and Bolin. And then Lin showed up all ticked off. She went on about how Su will never change and how she hated her. Korra and Bolin were watching from the side.

"You know what Lin I'm starting to see why Tenzin broke up with you." Lin narrowed her eyes at Su when she said that.

"That was a little cruel." Korra whispered to Bolin.

"Don't worry. Lin is already angry. There is nothing that Su can say that will set her off now." Bolin seemed very confident.

"Also I'm not surprised about Kya constantly going away from you." Korra and Bolin gasped at that comment and Lin growled and attacked Su.

"Should I stop them?" Korra asked looking at the two sisters.

"You don't have any siblings. Fighting is all a part of a healing process." Just then a giant boulder crashed between the two of them. "But we might wanna get further away from this healing process." Bolin and Korra bolted as everyone came to see what's going on. The two told them what happened. Then bits of rock and metal started flying everywhere.

Korra and Bolin made a wall to stop the rocks and metal bits. But out of nowhere a big ball of metal crashed through the wall and hit Asami. She was sent flying into the metal wall behind them and collapsing on the ground.

"Asami!" Korra shouted and the fighting stopped. Everyone rushed to the collapsed CEO. Korra was frozen for a few seconds but then she ran towards her and pushed everyone away from Asami using more force than she thought. Korra kneeled down next to Asami and wrapped her in her arms. "Asami! Asami! Come on! Open your eyes! Asami! Please!" Korra was more than freaking out right now, everyone was worried about Asami but Korra was on another level. They could see that Korra was clearly freaking out and it made everyone a bit confused. Even more so when tears started running down Korras face. "Asami... Please... You can't... You can't leave me..." Korra's eyes started glowing and a giant wind started to blow.

"She's gone into the Avatar State! What now?!" Bolin shouted as the wind threatened to blow them away.

But then something else happened that made them almost lose their balance. They saw Asami wrap her arms around Korra's neck and kiss her. Korra's eyes stopped glowing and she returned Asami's kiss while closing her eyes. When they separated Asami looked at Korra. "I'm sorry." Then she fainted in Korra's arms.

For a while there was silence. Then Su carefully approached them. "Korra we need to take her to a healer. Is that ok?" Korra merely nodded. "Wing, Wei could you carry her." The twins listened to their mother. Everyone followed them. Asami was in the infirmary while everyone else was in the other room.

Everyone was silent. Suddenly Mako stood up. "Ok will someone please explain what the hell is going on?"

Bolin attempted to calm his brother. "Easy bro, calm down. I don't think asking questions will help anyone now." Bolin looked at Korra who was sitting on a bench, hugging her knees to her chest. She was shaking a bit and her eyes looked empty but still very concerned. Mako huffed and went over to her.

"Korra!" Korra didn't react to his voice. Suddenly Mako grabbed the front of her shirt and pulled her up. "What the hell?! What's with the kiss?! Are you two together now or what?! Hey Korra, answer me!"

For a few seconds everything was silent.

"Just shut up for once. What the hell makes you think you have the right to talk to me like that huh?" Mako was a bit taken back at Korras tone of voice, his face showing both fear and anger. Korra looked him in the eye and Mako froze. He never saw Korra look so terrifying. "You think you know everything, don't you?! But you don't! You don't know a thing! Not about me and not about Asami! So shut up! Just shut up!" Korra hit Mako's chest with her fists but her blows were very weak.

A man stepped through the door. "Excuse me. Miss Sato is awake."

At those words Korra pushed Mako out of the way and ran into the room. She saw Asami sitting on a bed. "Asami!" Korra shouted and tackled Asami. She wrapped her arms around her as tears ran down her cheeks. "Thank Raava... You're ok... I was so worried..."

Asami smiled and hugged Korra. They sat up and looked into each other's eyes. "I'm sorry for worrying you." Asami pressed her forehead to Korra's.

"I'm so glad." Korra placed a hand on Asami's cheek. Asami hummed and nuzzled into her palm. A few moments after that they noticed they weren't alone. They looked towards the door and saw everyone looking at them. Mako worried them most of all.

Asami stopped smiling and looked at Korra. "I'm sorry. I blew our secret didn't I?"

Korra smiled. "It's alright. I don't care about that. All that matters is that you're safe." Korra wanted to kiss Asami so badly at that moment, but she held back because she didn't know how everyone would react. Instead she took her and in hers and smiled. "Alright." She turned to everyone. "I assume you all have a lot of questions. Let's get started then."

Over the next three hours Korra and Asami spent their time explaining to everyone what's been going on between them. For the most part the news was taken well. Mako was a bit angry at first but after a while he calmed down and accepted it.

Korra and Asami were happy that they didn't have to hide their relationship anymore and they were happy that they found each other. Together they would face many trials but they will always be with each other.

Story 4: Old enemies, familiar faces

Korra and Asami are back from their vacation and have yet to tell everyone about their new relationship. One night while out with their friends an old enemy pays a visit. An enemy of many faces.

Korra and Asami stepped out of the spirit portal with Korra's arm around Asami's waist and Asami's arm around Korra's shoulders.

"So after three weeks in the Spirit World we're finally back." Asami smiled and looked at Korra but Korra wasn't smiling. "Hey what's wrong?"

"I wanted to stay longer. Just the two of us. It was nice. Now that we're back we won't get to spend as much time together." Korra tightened her grip around Asami's waist.

"It'll be alright. Let's make sure we spend as much time with each other as possible." Asami saw Korra smile at that. "By the way what are we now?"

Korra looked at Asami with a big smile. "Girlfriends." She gave Asami a peck on the lips.

"I was hoping you would say that. I mean I'm no expert but I'm pretty sure friends don't make out." Asami smirked.

Korra smirked back. "I really will miss you. Especially hugging you at night. I'll be cold."

"Korra you grew up in the South Pole." Asami stated.

"Alright then. I'll be lonely." Korra responded and brought Asami's body closer to hers.

Asami blushed. "Then hug Naga."

"I don't want Naga. I don't want anybody but you." Asami couldn't miss the hint of sadness in Korra's voice.

Asami cupped Korras face and kissed her passionately. The kiss lasted until their lungs started burning for air.

"You could always come live with me." Asami whispered.

Korras eyes widened.

"You don't have to if you don't want to." Asami panicked.

"No! I do want to! But we agreed to keep our relationship a secret for a while. If I move in with you now it could be suspicious." Korra saw Asami's face when she said that and she could see the pain. Korra knew that it was hard for Asami to be alone, since she did lose her father and all. Even if Asami wouldn't say it Korra knew. "But I would like to stay with you tonight. I don't wanna sneak back to Air Temple Island at night."

Korra could see Asami's eyes lit up. Plus, the thought of spending an extra night with Asami in her arms filled her heart with joy. They walked through the streets and eventually reached Asami's house.

When they reached Asami's bedroom Korra realized she had never actually been in Asami's bedroom. And the fact that they were a couple now made her feel kind of nervous. Asami noticed that.

"Uh… We don't have to sleep in my room, we can…" Asami began but was cut off by a quick kiss from Korra.

"It's fine. It's just that… Being all alone with you in this house and in your bedroom… Kind of makes me wanna do stuff… If you know what I mean." Korra winked at Asami.

Asami blushed. When their relationship started Asami was kind of shocked at how bold Korra was at certain times. She could also be shy at times but still it made Asami wonder. Korra explained that Asami just made her feel that way. The thought that she was making Korra a bit of a pervert wasn't something Asami was totally against. Still sometimes she would still be shocked.

Asami opened the door and the two stepped in. "Make yourself at home. I'm just gonna get changed."

Korra turned around to give Asami her privacy. Even though Korra was so bold she still hadn't dared to look at Asami while she was undressing. It would be too much of a challenge for her to hold herself back if she did. Korra knew they still weren't ready to cross that one final line.

Korra took off her boots and her gloves. She also took off her shirt, leaving her only in her pants and a white undershirt.

"You can turn around now." Asami said.

Korra did turn around and she was stunned. Asami was standing there in a red, silk nightgown that just about reached her tights. Korra blushed, as did Asami when she realized that Korra was staring at her.

"Stop staring like that." Asami mumbled.

"That's kind of hard to do when you're so beautiful." Korra whispered.

Asami slowly stepped closer to Korra until they were inches apart. Asami didn't miss the lust in Korra's gaze. Korra took a deep breath and sat at the edge of Asami's bed. Asami sat down on Korra's lap with her tights at Korra's sides. Korra wrapped her arms around Asami and inhaled her scent.

Asami noticed Korra was shaking. He assumed it was because Korra had a harder time holding back her desires and lust than Asami did.

"Again?" Asami knew Korra experienced this thing before. It first happened in the Spirit World after they confessed their feelings for each other. Asami thinks that it might have something to do with Korra being the Avatar. Due to the high amount of spiritual energy Korra had a hard time dealing with suppressed sexual energy. Asami could see that it was painful. "Korra..."

"It's ok. I'm fine. Really." Korra looked up to Asami with a smile.

"But…" Asami began but was pulled down on the bed by Korra. She let out a tiny gasp when Korra hugged her tightly, bringing their bodies closer.

"Asami as long as I get to be with you I don't need anything else." Korra whispered.

Asami felt happy that Korra said that, yet she felt sad because she couldn't do anything for Korra right now. She just wrapped her arms around her and slowly drifted to sleep.

Over the next few days they had to catch up with work in the city and their friends as well. They kept their relationship a secret from their friends.

One day they decided to go spend a night out with their friends. It was a great night. Bolin and Opal talked about their relationship, Mako talked about his detective stuff, Tenzin talked about the possibilities of the new Spirit Portal, Bumi shared some old military tales, the Air siblings talked about what they were doing while Korra was in the South, Kya talked about the time she traveled the world and something about her… progressive relationship with Lin. It made Lin choke in her drink but Su apparently had some interesting comments about Kya and Lin as well.

Ultimately the night went well and everybody had a good time. They were walking through Avatar Korra Park when it happened. Korra felt a familiar evil presence.

"No one shows any emotion or you die." She warned. Everyone looked confused at first but then they saw a giant black centipede spirit with a white mask.

Koh the face stealer.

"Well what a surprise. Nice to see you again Avatar. And you came with another new face. How amusing." Koh circled around Korra. Mako and Bolin were ready to attack but Korra gave them the signal to stand down.

"I hoped I would never have to see you Koh." That statement made Koh laugh.

"I told you we would meet again. I never break my promises." Then Koh shifted his gaze to the others. He stopped when he saw Asami. "And what do we have here?"

Koh slowly made his way to Asami and was now looking directly at her. "My what a beautiful face you have. May I ask your name?"

"Asami Sato." Asami responded with a blank expression.

"Asami. A beautiful name for a beautiful woman. I would love to have your face in my collection." Koh started approaching Asami.

"Koh!" Korra shouted and turned around, her face was still blank but one couldn't miss the tone of her voice. "Go any closer and to her and I'll make you regret it."

Koh looked back and forth between Korra and Asami. "Ah I see. Lovers." Korra and Asami both flinched and they heard gasps around them. Koh started laughing. "This is way too good to be true! Tell me Asami did your precious Avatar tell you what happened to the previous Water Tribe Avatar's lover?"

"No she didn't." Asami still had a blank expression.

"I stole her face." This made Asami take a step back. "She was really beautiful. But I must say that you are even more beautiful." Koh turned back to Korra. "Tell me Avatar... Do all Avatars of the Water Tribe choose beautiful lovers or is it just you and Kuruk?"

Korra turned away. "Get away from Asami."

48

Koh smiled and in an instant made his way back to Korra. "You know when I took Ummi away from Kuruk not even he could keep a blank face. But I couldn't take his face because he was in the Avatar State. I wonder what expressions you would show me if I took your beloved woman away from you."

"That's easy." A small flame appeared in Korra's left hand. "I would kill you before you got anywhere near her." Korra had a killing look in her eyes.

"Yes! That's the look Kuruk had! Your eyes are the same as his! But he couldn't stop me eather! The sad part is that she believed in him! She believed in you! Until the very end Ummi believed that you would come save her!" His face changed to that of Ummi. "In the end she died all alone because you couldn't save her, but still Ummi believed in you!" Koh laughed while he was saying that.

"Shut up!" Korra shot a ball of flame at Koh but he dodged it. "Don't you talk about her! Don't you talk to me with her face!"

"Oh... scary... Does it anger you? That you couldn't save your lover in your past life? That the same might happen to your current lover?" Koh still had Ummi's face as he talked.

"I told you to shut up!" Korra shot another ball of fire at Koh but he vanished before she could hit him.

Korra fell to her knees. Everyone rushed to her side. Korra was crying. Asami came and hugged her. Korra returned her hug and wouldn't let go. "I'm sorry. I'm sorry. I'm so sorry. This wasn't supposed to happen. But I swear he won't touch you. No one will. Ever.

"Shhh. Its ok Korra." Asami tried to calm her down. Eventually she did. They all walked back to Asami's house. No one saying a word. They had a lot of explaining to do.

Story 5: The wedding

Taking place after season 4. Korra and Asami get married and say their vows to each other.

It was a beautiful day. The day of Korra and Asami's wedding. All of their friends were there. As well as Korra's parents. Bolin was doing the ceremony.

Asami wore a beautiful white dress. It had a hint of blue on the bottom. Korra was wearing a white tuxedo with the symbol of Raava and Vaatu on the back.

"I never thought this day would come." Bolin smiled. "I mean seriously who would have thought that these two would ever…" Bolin stopped when Korra sent him a dangerous glare. "But anyway… These two had their fair share of trials and ups and downs. But they overcame it all. Proving that true live really is a fickle creature. Hard to find, nearly impossible to tame. However, these two have done it." Bolin glanced at Korra between Korra and Asami before continuing. "Now for the vows. Asami?"

Asami smiled.

"Korra… I remember when I first saw you in the newspaper when I was a kid. Ever since then I've admired you and I wanted to be friends with you. When we meet I could hardly believe it was happening. I told myself that I will definitely become your friend. Not that you made it easy. Especially when you had a crush on my boyfriend." Asami paused while Korra and the rest of the crowd laughed. Except Mako who blushed in embarrassment. "However I still wanted to be your friend. And my wish came true. I actually got way more than I ever wished for. Thank you for that. I love you. And I always will. No matter how much time passes."

The couple smiled. Bolin choked a bit. "Korra? Your turn."

Korra nodded.

"Asami… When I first met you I didn't like you. But that wasn't your fault. It was mine. And of course who could ever forget that love triangle Mako crated." Korra looked towards Mako who blushed with embarrassment again. Then she looked back at Asami. "But even after all of that you were still there. After I was poisoned you never stopped trying to help me. When I went home to recover you wrote me almost every day. Asami if it weren't for you then I would have never recovered. You gave me strength. I decided I had to recover in order to come back to you. At that moment I realized that I love you. You became my reason for living. I love you Asami Sato. I will always love you. Forever and ever."

Bolin started crying. "That... That was so beautiful... You may now... You may now... I'm sorry I need a minute, you two go ahead and to the thing..." Bolin sobbed.

Korra and Asami smiled. Korra wrapped her arms around Asami's neck while Asami wrapped her arms around Korras neck. Their lips came together in a loving kiss. Korra took the opportunity and dipped her tongue in Asami's mouth making Asami moan. They disconnected their lips and heard clapping and chearing in the background. They knew that this was the beginning of their new life. A life they would built together.

The End

Printed in Poland
by Amazon Fulfillment
Poland Sp. z o.o., Wrocław